The Bungle in the Jungle

The Bungle in the Jungle

For Shirley, who has loved me just the way I am J.B.
For Anne and Pokneò, who lived through the Bungle P.G.

A Red Fox Book

Published by Random Century Children's Books
20 Vauxhall Bridge Road, London SW1V 2SA

A division of the Random Century Group
London Melbourne Sydney Auckland
Johannesburg and agencies throughout the world

First published by Hutchinson Children's Books 1989

Text © John Bush 1989
Illustrations © Paul Geraghty 1989

Red Fox edition 1992

Printed in Hong Kong
ISBN 0 09 966030 X

The Bungle in the Jungle

John Bush and Paul Geraghty

RED FOX

A merciless sun raged rampant at noon,
As waterwards wandered a thirsty baboon.
He staggered and teetered and started to totter,
In all of his days he'd never been hotter.

At the waterhole's edge he stretched out his lips
And sucked in that water in long, luscious sips.
Revived to his mischievous self by his drinking,
He saw his reflection, which started him thinking:

'I wonder why someone as clever as I
Should look so dull and drab to the eye?
How can I change that? Mmmm, let me see.
Got it! A sign on the baobab tree!'

BORED WITH YOUR LOOKS? WANT SOMETHING NEW?
MEET HERE TOMORROW AT DAWN IF YOU DO.

That's what he painted. That's what it said.
That's what everyone passing by read.

The fingers of dawn had scarce touched the sky
When a host of animals all gathered nigh.

'Friends,' said Baboon, 'good morning to you.
I presume you'd all like to wear something new?

'I've an upside-down tortoise which, as you know,
Can magic whatever we wish to be so.
Swapping our looks would be easy to do!
Ostrich, my friend, may I swap with you?

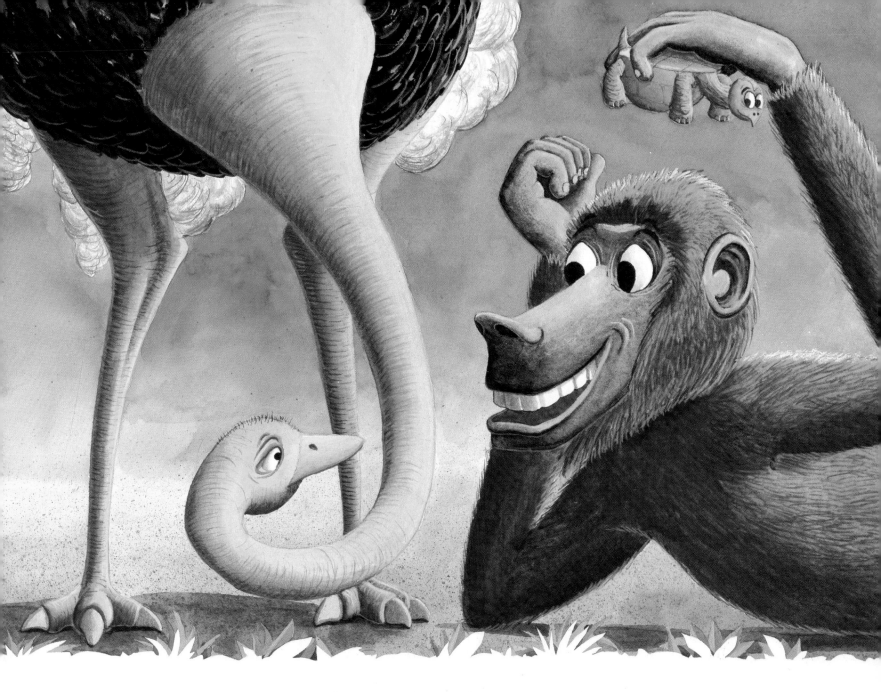

'Dare to be dashing, put on my fur.
Think on it, Ostrich. Consider it, sir.
Although in those feathers I'd look less refined,
If *you'd* like to change, I really don't mind.'

Ostrich and feathers were very soon parted,
With that all the swapping and switching was started.
'Rhino, old chap,' Buffalo said,
'Imagine my horns on the sides of your head.

'Swap me for those on the front of your face,
To tell you the truth, they look out of place.'
Rhino reflected, then shouted, 'Why not!
Undo 'em, unglue 'em, unscrew 'em, let's swap!'

Then up snorted Warthog, 'Who'd like my warts?'
Sniggers and jeers were the only retorts.

Giraffe and Lion swapped spots for mane.
Now Lion was spotty; Giraffe, hairy and plain.

Then up snorted Warthog, 'My tusks are for taking.'
But that was a swap that no one was making.

'My stripes for your spots. I'll help you arrange them,'
Said Zebra to Leopard, who answered, 'Exchange them!'

Then up snorted Warthog in his loudest voice:
'Who wants my tail? Speak up for first choice!
There's no finer tail in jungle or town;
When you run it stands up, when you stand it goes down!'

But no one took first choice, second or third,
Giggles and titters were all Warthog heard.
'Now,' said Baboon, 'it's time for inspection.
At the waterhole's edge you can see your reflection.'

Down at the waterhole's edge, one by one,
They peered in and cried, 'Oh, what have we done?'

There were grunts and roars and screeches of fright.
'Baboon,' they wailed, 'we must wish ourselves right!
That upside-down tortoise, where is he, we need him?'

'Friends,' he replied, 'I am sorry, I freed him.'

And in their stunned silence, they heard Warthog say,
'I think a warthog looks perfect this way.

'Truth to tell, such distinctive features
Make us the most unique of creatures.'

The others lamented the looks they had lost,
'See,' they exclaimed, 'what our vanity's cost!'
And four summers passed till those animals found
That upside-down tortoise to change things around.